OLIVIA™
and the Kite Party

adapted by Alex Harvey
based on the screenplay "Kite Season" written by Jack Monaco
illustrated by Patrick Spaziante

Ready-to-Read

Simon Spotlight
New York   London   Toronto   Sydney   New Delhi

Based on the TV series *OLIVIA*™ as seen on Nickelodeon™

SIMON SPOTLIGHT
An imprint of Simon & Schuster Children's Publishing Division
1230 Avenue of the Americas, New York, New York 10020
OLIVIA™ Ian Falconer Ink Unlimited, Inc. and © 2012 Ian Falconer and Classic Media, LLC
All rights reserved, including the right of reproduction in whole or in part in any form.
SIMON SPOTLIGHT, READY-TO-READ, and colophon are registered trademarks of Simon & Schuster, Inc.
For information about special discounts for bulk purchases, please contact Simon & Schuster Special
Sales at 1-866-506-1949 or business@simonandschuster.com.
Manufactured in the United States of America 0513 LAK
2 3 4 5 6 7 8 9 10
ISBN 978-1-4424-4649-6 (pbk)
ISBN 978-1-4424-4650-2 (hc)
ISBN 978-1-4424-4651-9 (eBook)

Whoosh!
It is a very windy day.
Olivia smiles.
It is a perfect day
to fly kites!

"Mom, do you have anything we can use to make kites?" Olivia asks.

"Well," Mom says. "We have ribbons, streamers, and bows. I do not know how you can make a kite out of them."

"Leave that to me,"
Olivia says.

After a while Ian says,
"I am done."
"Very nice," Olivia tells him.
"Are you ready to try it out?"

"But we need string,"
Ian says.

Olivia asks Francine for help.

"I have something even
better," Francine says.

"Yarn!"

"Do you want to make a kite?" Olivia asks Francine.
"There is enough wind for one hundred kites. It could be a party!"

Francine is excited.
"A kite party!" she says.

On pieces of paper,
Olivia writes:
"You are invited to our
kite party . . ."

When she is done,
she folds the papers into
paper airplanes . . .
and sends them flying out
the window!

Later, everyone gathers
with their kites.
"Great kites!" Olivia says.
"Is everybody ready?"
"Ready!" everyone says.

But Daisy has no kite.
"Where is yours, Daisy?"
asks Olivia.
"At home," Daisy says.
"There is no wind!"

Olivia looks around.
"Where did the wind go?"
she asks.
"Maybe the wind blew the
wind away," Ian says.

"I guess we will just have to
save the kites for another
day," says Mom.
"Sorry, Olivia, no wind,
no kites," Francine adds.

"Wait, so what if there is
no wind?" Olivia asks.
"We made our own kites.
Now you want us to
make it windy?" Daisy asks.

"We can all blow air!"
Ian says.
Everyone blows, but
nothing happens.
"We are not windy enough,"
says Ian.

"We just need to think bigger,"
Olivia says. "Much bigger."
Now everyone has a paper fan.
They start waving when Olivia
tells them to.

"And one, and two . . ."
But it does not work.
Olivia thinks.
"There is only one thing to do.
Think WAY bigger!" she says.

A short time later,
Olivia and Ian create
a windmill using a teepee,
canoe paddles, fans,
and a bicycle!

Ian starts to pedal.

"It is working!" Olivia shouts.

"We have wind!"

"I do not think I have seen so many kites in the sky," Mom says.
"Looks like yours is ready," Dad tells Olivia.

"It just needs
one more thing,"
Olivia says.
She adds a big red O
to her kite.

"Now it is perfect!"
says Olivia.
She lets go of the kite
and it flies high in the sky!